The Only Dog is a Wheaten Terrier

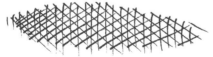

Written & illustrated
by David Bell

Before you get into this story, Feiyan
says that if you're thinking of getting
a new dog, especially a puppy, to look for one
that's happy and healthy. So only talk to loving,
caring, registered breeders who do health tests.
Bringing a dog into your life is a big responsibility,
but doing things properly means you'll have
a best friend forever.

The Only Dog is a Wheaten Terrier

Text set in Baskerville. So you could say Baskerville of the hound.

For Shelley Lyons Borenstein & Jameson,
Lynn Nielsen Kasics & Sherlock, Laurel Brunke & Padraig & Ruaírí,
Terry and Ashley Lynne Ulrich & Ellie, Rick Gagliardi & Wilson,
Renee Lynn & Rowan, Christine Tokyo & Mugi, Lisa Sullivan & Geronimo,
Donna Slentz Cripe & Luc, Buffy Hatcher Brown Oliver & Olivia,
Celeste Uresti & Harper, Betsy Zesinger Ingraham & Maury,
Angela Carlaw & Lulu, Susan Paige & Kirby, Michael Adams & Rocco-Morocco,
Cheryl Willmon Henke & Booker, Denise Barron Potter & Finn,
Lauren Edwards Hassig & Bailey, Jessica Lavergne,
Alison Moore Jeske & Bruno, Shyna Pina & Lin, G Seidman Miller & Echo,
Chelsea Ramon & Decklan, Sue Roeder, Alicia Strawser & Dobby,
Scott-Ellen Rubin Dornfeld & Harper, Tara Zimmerman & Isolde, Ruby McGrane
Druiventak & Riley, Navarrete Genesis & Zacapi & Nuvo & Jack,
Kathleen Doyle-White, Courtney Scholl, Nedra Post & Kona,
Deb Cappo Maalona & Benji, Jennifer Martin & Jax, Debbie and Kodiak,
Marianne Kantor Sesselman & Teddy, Karen Webster & Kate,
Keri McKenna Lonieski & Molly, Tiffany Nguyen & Lilo, Dorothy Bloom & Shani,
Kerily McEvoy & Cooper, Susan Paige & Kirby, Mike Wight & Molly,
Joan Biggar & Oscar, Lindsay Orioles & Maggie Maeve, Sarah Chapman &
Bourke, Pamela Lofgren Luria & Charleston, Robin Eschell & King George ll,
Joe Kolakowski & Bella, Steve Feldman & Sir Casey & Bailey,
Thea Du Toit & Nora, Teresa Kirke & Finn, Heidi Baldwin & Kadie Peachbear,
Patricia Bove Doria & Maggie, Alesia Rothfuss Milam & Cooper,
Carolyn Elsworthy & Harry, Callie Marion, Erin Lambert Bree & Bailey,
Kathy Taylor, Retta Carr Saenz & Ella, Michelle Stoker Valen & Boddie & Daisy,
Wayne King & Charlie, Holly Ross and Kevin & Bentley,
everyone in the Wheaten Greetin' Facebook Group,
and all lovers of Wheaten Terriers.

I want, I demand, by the end of this month,

A dog that resembles a python,

That'll squirm on the floor,

But not on all fours,

And can squeeze all the fleas off a lion.

Or maybe perhaps, a new dog for next week?

A dog that can fly like a seagull?

That can catch a fat sparrow,

Or maybe an arrow,

Or even a great golden eagle.

Even better for me is a dog by tomorrow,

A dog that can hide among penguins.

In its black and white suit,

And its pointed-up snoot,

They'll be fooled into thinking it's genuine.

I was passing your place, and wished on a whim,

For an elephant dog. By this evening?

As big as three boats,

With a prehensile nose,

I can wrap all around me to lie in.

Your majesty? What? *Another* new dog?

A *jaguar* dog? In two hours?

That can leap forty feet,

From a baobab tree,

To scare birds off my pood-upon towers.

You want me to dish up a dog that's a *fish*?

By the time it begins to go dark?

With fins like a carp.

And who swims like a shark.

And makes bubbles instead of a bark.

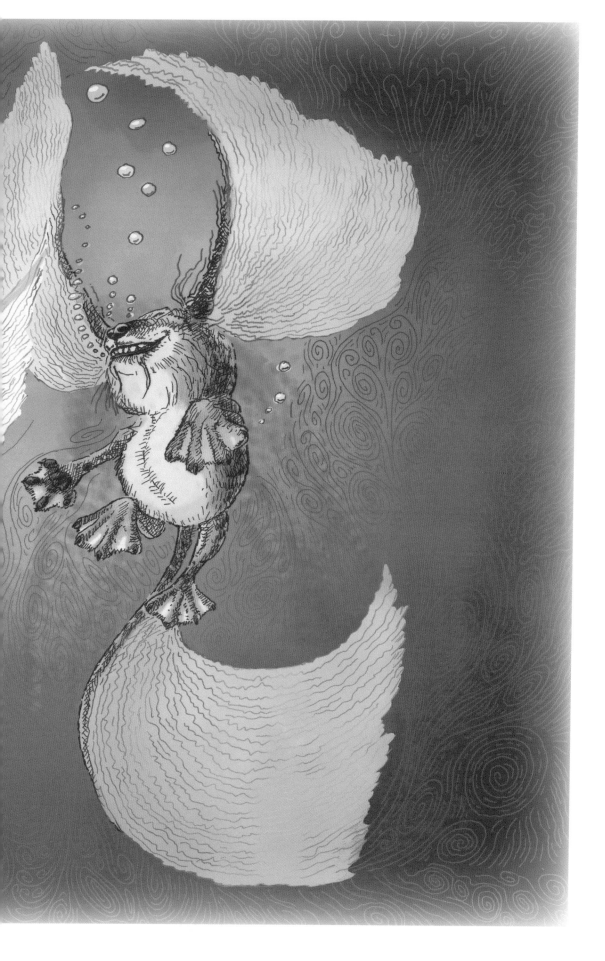

What I don't understand is, if you want a dog,

Why on earth make it look like a bison?

Or a sheep, or a hake,

Or a three-headed snake,

Or a miniature fire-breathing dragon?

Look over here: a Wheaten Terrier

They're the dog that you want for a friend-

A bullet of muscle,

And bustling snuffles,

Aimed straight at your heart 'til the end.

The Mole dog, from 'The Dog Army'

The Smuggler dog, from 'The Dog Assassins'

The Otter dog, from 'The Dog Hunters'

The Adventures of Llewelyn and Gelert

Written and illustrated by David Bell

Available on Amazon

Printed in Great Britain
by Amazon